Shapes

Karen Bryant-Mole Edited by Jenny Tyler

Illustrated by Graham Round

About this book

This book is designed for an adult and child
to use together. It introduces young children to
both two-dimensional and three-dimensional
shapes. As well as naming the shapes, there
are lots of matching and sorting activities which
help children develop the ability to recognize
and discriminate between shapes. The book
makes a variety of practical suggestions for
activities that can be done at home.

The book also includes a shape game that
can be played over and over again.

Notes for parents

It is best to use this book when both you and your child are in the right mood to enjoy it. Try not to do too much at any one time. If your child seems unready or unwilling to tackle any of the activities, just leave it and come back to it later.

Working order

This book covers both 2-dimensional (2D) and 3-dimensional (3D) shapes. Young children are usually more familiar with the names of 2D shapes, so these are looked at first. If you prefer, however, you could introduce 3D shapes first by starting at page 14 and working through to page 22. Follow this with pages 3 to 13 and, finally, complete pages 23 and 24.

Shape names

The 2D shapes looked at in this book are circle, square, rectangle and triangle. The 3D shapes are sphere, cylinder, cube and cuboid. "Cuboid" is not a word used by most of us in everyday conversation but it is the term used in most schools to describe a brick-type shape and for this reason is used in this book.

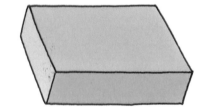

A typical cuboid.

The adjectives circular, triangular and rectangular have also been used in this book. If you feel that these will confuse your child, you could use a phrase such as "shaped like a triangle" instead.

As well as introducing the names of the shapes, the activities in this book also help your child to match, sort and discriminate between shapes. In the final pages the relationship between 2D and 3D shapes is explored by looking at the 3D shapes and their 2D faces.

Handling shapes

At this early stage, shape, particularly 3D shape, should involve lots of practical experiences. Some practical suggestions are made in this book which involve finding examples of 3D shapes to look at and feel. Try to include these if you can as handling the shapes is the best way of understanding them and their properties.

Other activities

Many of the activities that cat and mouse are doing in the book, such as printing and making brick constructions, could be done at home. By copying cat and mouse you will increase the value of the activities on the page and help your child to gain a much richer understanding of the concept of shape.

You can extend your child's experiences with lots of other types of activities too. Instead of throwing away toothpaste boxes and empty tea packets, save them and use them to make "junk" models.

You can make spheres from playdough or you can roll out the dough very thinly and use plastic knives or shape cutters to make squares or triangles.

Encourage your child to notice shapes all around her. Always use the correct term to describe them and make sure that neither of you falls into the trap of calling a 3D shape by a 2D name. A football is a sphere remember, not a circle.

Pens and pencils

There are plenty of coloring opportunities in this book and your child will need a set of crayons or felt pens for these. Coloring is a valuable way of helping develop good pencil control. Before you start, make sure your child is holding the pen or pencil correctly. It is easy to develop bad writing habits with the wrong grip.

Pens and pencils should be held lightly between the thumb and first two fingers, about 1 in from the point.

Circles

- Color in the insides of all the circles in this picture with red.

- Finish coloring the picture with other colors.

Squares

A **square** has 4 sides and 4 corners. All the sides are the same length.

Help me by drawing over the colored lines to make 5 squares.

- The animals are hanging up flags.

- Color all the square ones.

Rectangles

A **rectangle** has 4 sides and 4 corners like a square…

…but each pair of sides is a different length.

Help us draw some rectangles by drawing over the gray lines with colored pens.

- Cat and mouse are trying to decide which windows and doors are rectangles and which are squares.

- Help them by coloring the rectangles yellow and squares blue.

To check if a shape is a square, turn the book sideways. If it looks exactly the same, it is a square.

5

Triangles

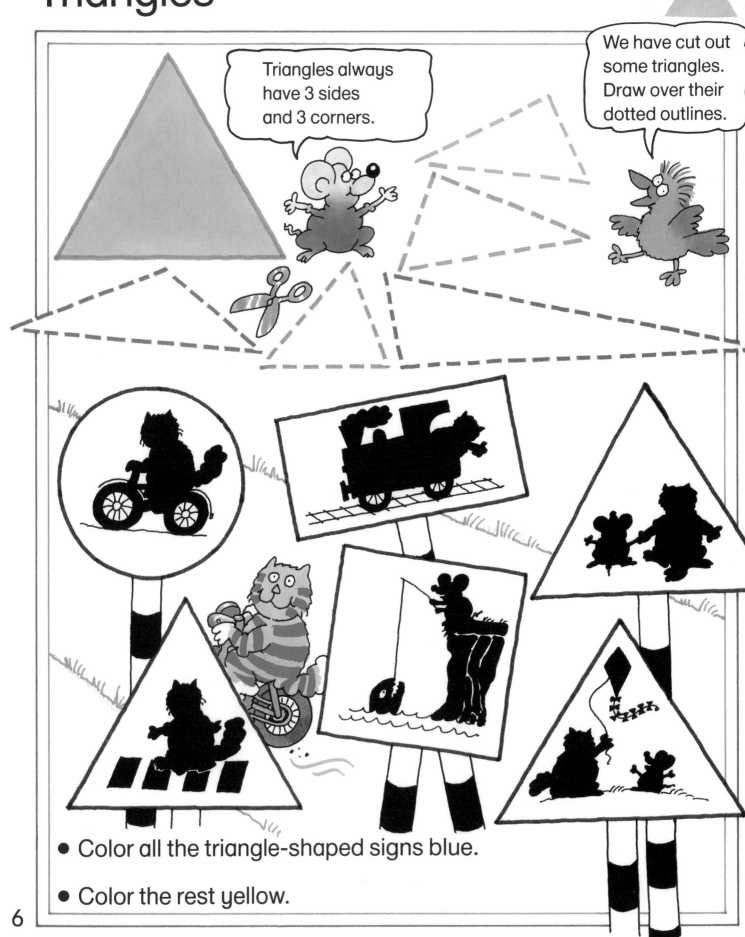

Triangles always have 3 sides and 3 corners.

We have cut out some triangles. Draw over their dotted outlines.

- Color all the triangle-shaped signs blue.

- Color the rest yellow.

6

Kite shapes

- Cat, mouse, frog and elephant are flying their kites.
  What shape are the kites?

- Each animal has a shape on his jumper which matches his kite.
  Draw in the kite strings to join each kite to its owner.
  Color each kite to match its owners jumper.

7

Frog's shop

Cat and mouse are visiting frog's shop.

- Color all the triangles purple.

- Color all the circles orange.

- Color all the squares yellow.

- Color all the rectangles green.

- What shape things have cat and mouse bought?

8

Mouse's pictures

- Mouse is showing cat his new pictures. What shape are they?

- Who can you see in the square picture? Color him pink.

- Who can you see in the picture shaped like a rectangle? Color him green.

- What does the circular picture show?

- What shape is the picture of the duck?

Sticker collections

Cat, mouse, frog and pig are sorting out their stickers. They each collect one shape of sticker.

- Find out which shape each animal collects by looking at the front of his sticker album.

- Draw lines to join each sticker to the correct book.

- Color the stickers to match the shape on the front of the book.

Spiders' houses

Follow the strands to find out where each spider lives.

Color the spider who lives in the circular house purple.

Color the spider who lives in the square house orange.

Color the spider who lives in the triangular house red.

Color the spider who lives in the rectangular house green.

Color the front doors to match the spider who lives there.

Shape game

- You will need 24 markers or pieces of cardboard and a dice.
- Cover the dice with squares of white sticky paper.
  Color one side red and one side green.
  Draw a triangle, a square, a rectangle and a
  circle on the other sides.
- Decide which player will be cat and which will be mouse. Cat
  will cover the red shapes. Mouse will cover the yellow shapes.

- Take turns rolling the dice.

- If you roll a shape, put a marker on that shape on your picture.

- If you roll a red, you miss a turn.
  If you roll a green, you take another turn.

- The winner is the first to cover all 12 shapes.

Spheres

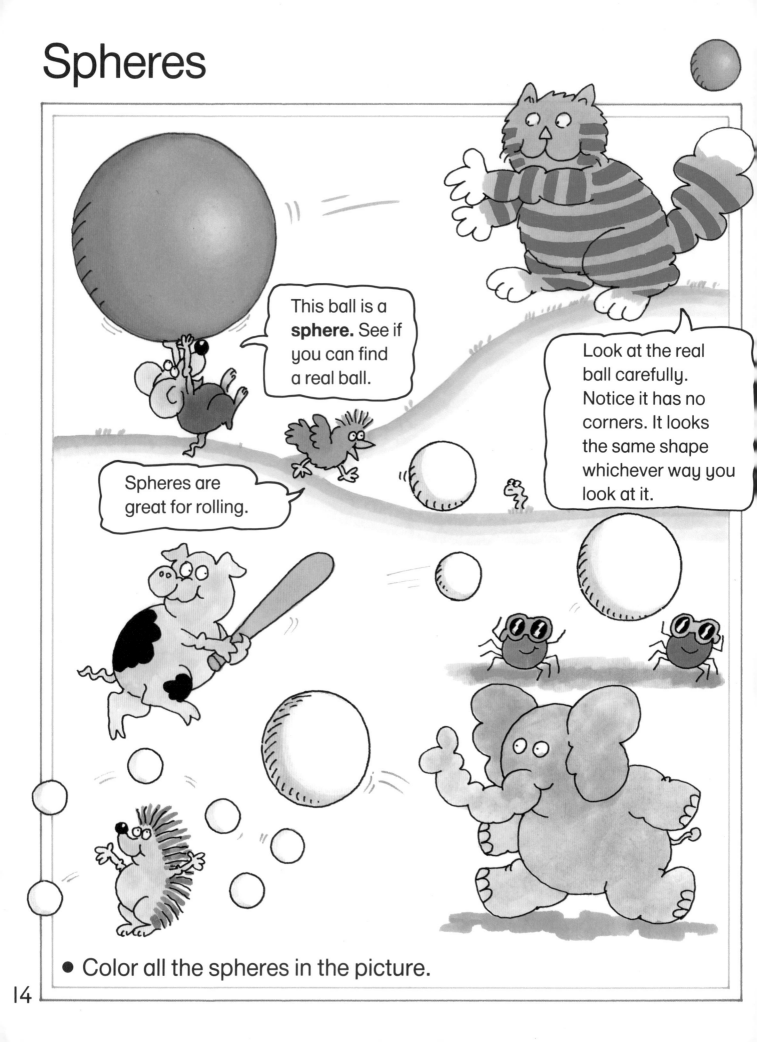

This ball is a **sphere.** See if you can find a real ball.

Look at the real ball carefully. Notice it has no corners. It looks the same shape whichever way you look at it.

Spheres are great for rolling.

● Color all the spheres in the picture.

14

Cylinders

- Color the sea lions balancing cylinders on their noses blue.

- Color the sea lions balancing spheres on their noses green.

- What is frog balancing on his head?

Cubes

This is a **cube.** All its sides are the same size.

Cubes are good for building.

Find a cube-shaped brick. How many sides has it got?

● The clown is juggling. Color his large cubes orange and his small cubes purple.

Cuboids

- It is mouse's birthday. Some of his presents are cubes. Color them yellow.

- Some are cuboids. Color them red.

- What shape are his other presents?

Building bricks

- Cat, mouse and frog are playing with their building bricks.

- What shapes have they used?

- Can you work out which of these groups of bricks cat used to build his tower?
Color the bricks to match the bricks in cat's tower.

- Do the same for mouse's bridge and frog's wall.

Tidying up

- Cat, mouse and frog are putting the bricks away.
  Each shape goes in a different box.

- There is a label on each box to show which shape belongs in it.
  Help the animals by drawing a line from each brick to its box.

- Color each brick the same color as the shape on its box.

Shopping shapes

- Cat, mouse and frog are at the supermarket.

- Some things have not been colored. Can you color them using this code.

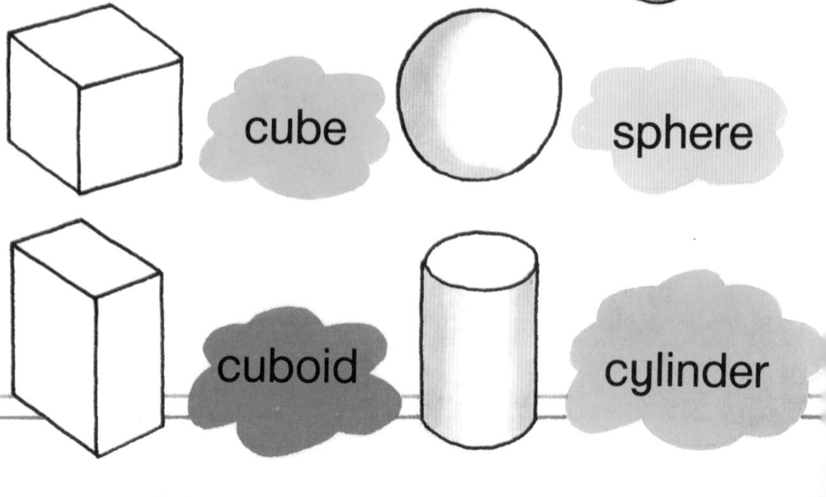

cube

sphere

cuboid

cylinder

- What do you think will happen if mouse takes the can away? Find some cylinder bricks and try it yourself.

- Look in your cupboards at home. How many cubes, cuboids and cylinders can you find?

- Look for these shapes next time you go shopping.

Hidden shapes

- Mouse has hidden 3 cylinders, 3 spheres, 3 cubes and
  3 cuboids around the room.
  Cat is trying to find them. Can you help?

- When you find one, color one of the matching shapes below
  in the same color as the shape you have found.

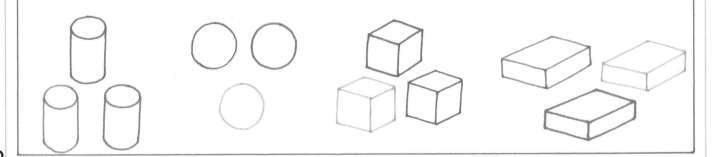

Printing shapes

- Cat and mouse are using blocks to do some printing.

- What shape has mouse printed with his cube?
  Color all the shapes printed with the cube red.

- What shape has cat printed with his cylinder?
  Color all the shapes printed with the cylinder blue.

- What shape has the cuboid made?
  Color all the shapes printed with the cuboid yellow.

- What do you think made the prints on the table?

Postman cat

- Look at the letterboxes on each door. What shape are they?

- Help cat decide which letterbox each parcel will go through.

- Color each parcel the same color as the door it should go through.